To my parents and grandparents, aunts and uncles,
brothers and sisters, nieces and nephews and cousins,
and who they have become and are becoming
—V.M.N.

For Isaiah, Ginger, and all of their little cousins—
Akira, Noel, Zachary, Chloe, Ryan, Owen, Eitan,
Talia, Zoe, Ava, Jane, Ariella, and Langston
—S.Q.

Published in the United States by Random House Children's Books,
a division of Random House, Inc., New York.

Library of Congress Cataloging-in-Publication Data
Nelson, Vaunda Micheaux.
Who will I be, Lord? / by Vaunda Micheaux Nelson ; illustrated by Sean Qualls. — 1st ed.
p. cm.
Summary: A young girl recalls the stories she has been told about the members of her family and wonders what kind of person she will become.
ISBN 978-0-375-84342-6 (trade) — ISBN 978-0-375-94342-3 (lib. bdg.)
1. African Americans—Juvenile fiction. [1. African Americans—Fiction. 2. Racially mixed people—Fiction. 3. Identity—Fiction. 4. Christian life—Fiction.] I. Qualls, Sean, ill. II. Title.
PZ7.N43773Wh 2009
[E]—dc22 2008035186

MANUFACTURED IN CHINA 10 9 8 7 6 5 4 3 2 1 First Edition

WHO WILL I BE, LORD?

BY VAUNDA MICHEAUX NELSON
ILLUSTRATED BY SEAN QUALLS

Random House New York

Great-Grandpap was a mailman. He knew everybody in town and everybody knew him.

On weekends, Great-Grandpap played banjo with Schultz's Nighthawks on WNBO Radio, before there was even television.

People said Great-Grandpap loved music. Mama says he loved Great-Grandma more. He gave up the band when their kids were born and made music with *them* on Saturday nights instead. "Nothin's more important than family," he'd say. Mama says he learned that from his own grandpa, who was a slave.

Great-Grandpap was a mailman.

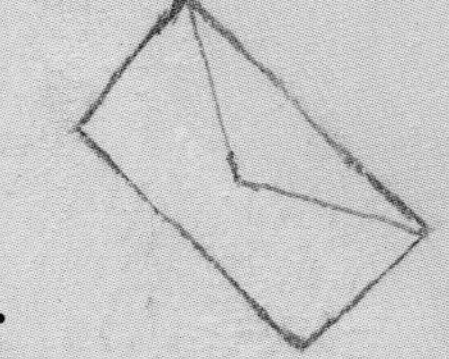

And what will I be, Lord?

What will I be?

Great-Grandma was a housewife. She mama'd five children and made the best cakes in the county. She wore pants when other ladies mostly only wore dresses.

Great-Grandma was white and she married my great-grandpap. After the wedding, her mama and papa said they didn't have a daughter. Great-Grandma never saw them again. People said she was crazy. Mama says, "She *was* crazy—crazy about Pap!" Mama says Great-Grandma knew more about love than most folks.

Great-Grandma
was a housewife.

And what will I be, Lord? What will I be?

My grampa is a preacher. Every week we all go to Bethel A.M.E. Church for Sunday school, then morning services and Grampa's sermon. Of all the lessons he's learned, Grampa says the Golden Rule is the one that could save everybody. "Just treat other people the way you want to be treated." Grampa says he learned that from his mama, who would feed a stranger just for knocking on her door.

People say Grampa's preachin' has quiet power.

Mama says that's because Grampa doesn't holler his sermons. His voice is nice and soft, but his words talk loud. When Grampa whispers "amen," Mama says it thunders clear up to Heaven.

My grampa is a preacher.

And what will I be, Lord? What will I be?

My grandma is a teacher. You have to be real smart to be one. When I don't want to go to school, Grandma shakes her head and says, "It's a shame." Then she starts tellin' her old stories about slavery, when people were whipped or killed for learning to read. Grandma says it ain't right. (But she doesn't say "ain't.")

People say Grandma's "uppity" because she's always correcting somebody's way of talking. Mama says Grandma's proud of her education and likes passing the plate around so everybody can have some.

My grandma is a teacher.

And what will I be, Lord? What will I be?

My uncle is a pool shark.

He makes his money playin' eight ball.
He handles a pool cue like a magic
wand and makes the colored balls
dance on the table.

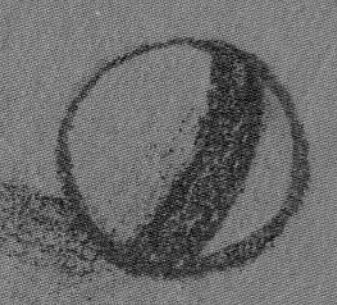

When Uncle comes to visit, he sits me on his lap and says, "If you're gonna be a ditchdigger, learn to dig the best ditches on this earth." Then he reaches in his pocket and gives me a cinnamon candy that makes my tongue red hot.

People say he's a rascal.
Mama says she likes him
because he isn't two-faced
like some. He is who he is.

My uncle is a pool shark.

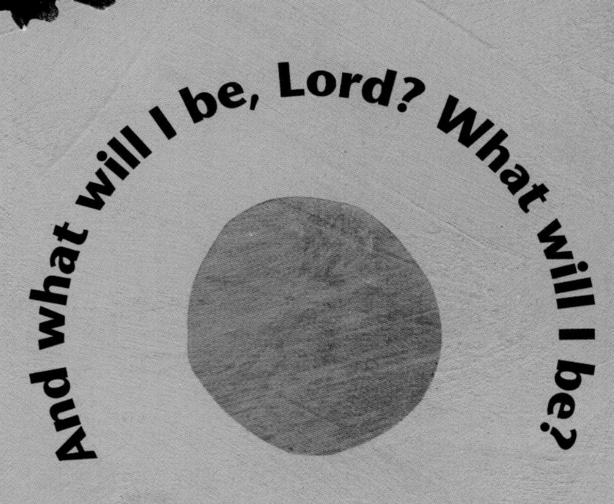

And what will I be, Lord? What will I be?

My cousin is a jazzman.
He plays blues piano and writes
soulful songs about love. When
he makes music, my whole body
bobs to the beat all by itself.
I can't stop it.

My cousin says he's going to be famous someday. He isn't famous yet, so he works at Dizzy's Diner, flipping burgers. When he gets home from Dizzy's, my cousin sits at his keyboard and plays and plays and plays.

People say he's a dreamer. Mama says he has a heart full of passion. She says dreaming and believing put him halfway there. What matters is the trying.

My cousin is a jazzman.

And what will I be, Lord? What will I be?

My papa is a car man. He makes dented doors and crumpled fenders look brand-new. His shop always smells like paint, and he has to wear a safety mask.

When Papa comes home from work, he washes his hands with Lava soap, takes off his big work boots, and stretches out on the living room rug. His feet are a little stinky, but that's okay. I curl up beside him, and we rest till Mama calls us for supper.

If a customer can't afford his work, Papa says, "Pay me when you can." Almost everybody in town owes Papa money. Some people say that's bad business. Mama says, "*Some* people oughta mind their *own* business." She says Papa is like someone from Great-Grandpap's time, when neighbors helped each other and a handshake was enough.

My papa is a car man.

And what will I be, Lord? What will I be?

My mama is a mama.
Seems like she takes care of everybody. On Fridays she drives Mrs. Rogers, who's almost blind, to the beauty parlor. Mama visits old Mr. Harris at the nursing home every Tuesday. She'll help my auntie paint her porch, then come home and make bread pudding with lemon sauce especially for Papa.

Mama slips notes inside my lunch box that make me laugh or just feel good. And she tells me stories about our family. Most times it's the same ones over, but I still like them.

People say Mama was born with a talent for lookin' after folks. Mama says talent has more to do with workin' hard than with what comes natural. She says God gives us each some seeds to sow.

The rest is up to us.

My mama is a mama.
And what will I be, Lord? **Who** will I be?
I guess like Mama says, it's up to me.